THE KITCHEN TALKS

POEMS BY
Shirley Mozelle

ILLUSTRATIONS BY
Petra Mathers

Henry Holt and Company
New York

THE KITCHEN TALKS
An Up-Close Personal Interview

I have my sizzles,
My crackles,
My bubbles,
My pops,

My swooshes and swishes,
Hums, rings, and buzzes,
Klunks, thumps,
Whistles and tickles and whirls.

Ticks and tocks,
Happy chatter, quiet talks,
Sneaks and peeks,
Bites and drinks,

Lunches, breakfast, dinner,
Brunches, buffets, parties—
Surprise! Surprise!
Kisses, hugs, meows, purrs,

Midnight snacks,
Midnight dreams . . .

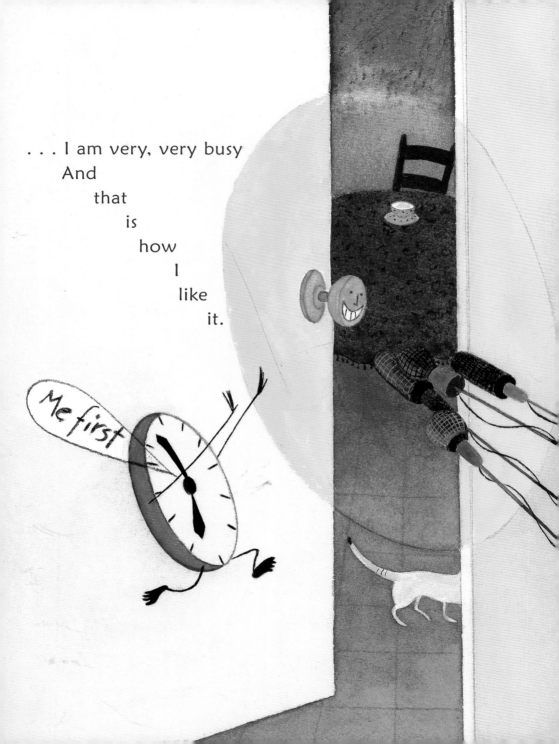

. . . I am very, very busy
And
        that
            is
                how
                    I
                        like
                            it.

Me first

KITCHEN CLOCK

Tick-tock
The kitchen clock.
Got a minute
In my pocket.

Twelve, one, two.
Ticks for me,
Tocks for you.

Kitchen clock
On the wall,
Blue wall—
Tick-tock.

TOASTER

Jack-in-the-box
For bread
Includes a tan.

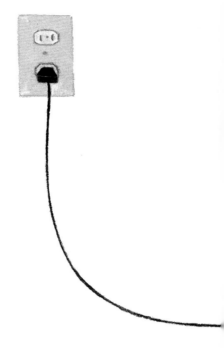

FAVORITE CUP

Not that one,

Not that one,

Not that one.

That's the one!

CREAMER

The cow is a dreamer.
How else could she have jumped over the moon?

REFRIGERATOR

My door
      Opens
  Closes
      Opens
  Closes
      Opens
  Closes—
You know the routine.

Still,
As a rule,
I keep my C O O L .

KITCHEN MAGNETS

Stick to the refrigerator—
Hold pictures and numbers,
Reminders and quotes,
Or special notes.
My favorite?

I LOVE YOU.

FREEZER

Cold as ice
But no goose bumps.

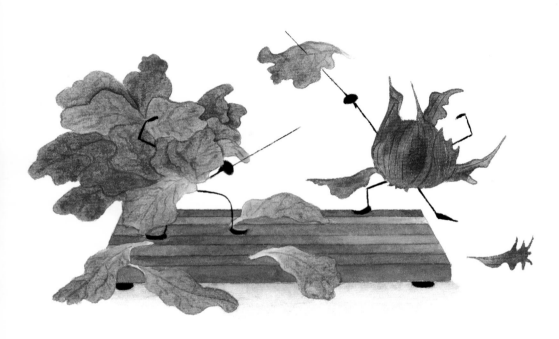

CUTTING BOARD

Chop-chop,
Slice,
Dice,

Onion, lettuce cut up.

CAN OPENER

Hummm . . .
Rummm . . .
Round and round
On the cutting edge.

The cat cannot resist
This sound.

STOVE
Electrically Speaking

Bubble
Boil
Crackle
Fry

Nice and quiet
Broil or bake

Either way,
I cook with coils.

I can handle hot.
I do, a lot.

But some days
I dream of cool—

A breeze,
A wave,
A cube,

A sip or two.

ROLLING PIN

Back and forth
Forth and back
It does not matter—
I take what is FAT
And make it FLATTER.

COOKIE JAR

When I am full—
Chocolate chip,
Butter pecan,
Coconut—
Everyone loves me.

When I am empty
(And I hate the feeling),
No one is around.

WASHING DISHES

Bubble up,
Scrub them up,
Wash, wash, wash.
Plates, cups . . .

Oops, flying saucers!

PAPER TOWELS

One for the hands,
One for the grease,
One for the spills . . .

. . . Don't stop me now—I'm on a roll.

SILVERWARE

When the mood hits
It's hup, two, three, four,
Out of the drawer.

The spoon,
The fork,
The knife—
They like a little nightlife.

60 WATTS

The spoon's moon
Is round and bright.
The spoon's moon
Is the ceiling light.

FAUCET

Drip   Drop
Drop   Drip

                        Plumber, please!

CURTAINS

The curtains
See the window,
The window
Sees the day,
The day
Sees the night,
The night
Sees the stars,
The stars
See the moon,
The moon
Sees the window,
The window
Sees the curtains.

For Nina Ignatowicz, Robin Tordini,
Petra Mathers, and Aunt Ezelle,
whose kitchen has been a blessing
(thanks, too, to Amy and Laurent)
—S. M.

To Donalda, queen of desserts
—P. M.

Henry Holt and Company, LLC, *Publishers since 1866*
175 Fifth Avenue, New York, New York 10010
www.henryholtchildrensbooks.com

Henry Holt® is a registered trademark of Henry Holt and Company, LLC.
Text copyright © 2006 by Shirley Mozelle
Illustrations copyright © 2006 by Petra Mathers
All rights reserved. Distributed in Canada by H. B. Fenn and Company Ltd.

Library of Congress Cataloging-in-Publication Data
Mozelle, Shirley.
The kitchen talks / by Shirley Mozelle ; illustrated by Petra Mathers.
        p.   cm.
ISBN-13: 978-0-8050-7143-6 / ISBN-10: 0-8050-7143-1
1. Kitchens—Juvenile poetry. 2. Kitchen utensils—Juvenile poetry.
3. Kitchen appliances—Juvenile poetry. 4. Children's poetry, American.
I. Mathers, Petra, ill. II. Title.
PS3563.O97K58 2006   811'.54—dc22   2005012172

First Edition—2006 / Designed by Laurent Linn
The artist used watercolor to create the illustrations for this book.
Printed in the United States of America
on acid-free paper. ∞

1 3 5 7 9 10 8 6 4 2